Ratio Holmes

and the
Case of the Blue Stripe Vandal

D0395661

Keystone Canyon Press
2341 Crestone Drive
Reno, NV 89523

www.keystonecanyon.com

Publisher Alrica Goldstein
Copyeditor Sylvan Baker
Cover Designer Pandowo Limo

A Cataloging-in-Publication record for this title is available from the Library of Congress.

ISBN 978-1-953055-12-5
EPUB ISBN 978-1-953055-13-2

Manufactured in the United States of America

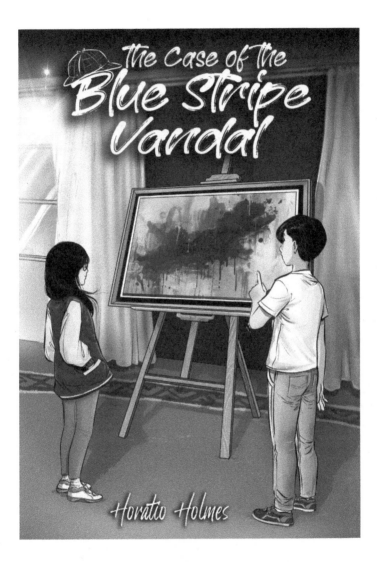

The Case of the Blue Stripe Vandal

Horatio Holmes

KEYSTONE
CANYON PRESS

To Anuroopa who might say "aht"
in her purple turtleneck. I'm a fan.

Meet Ratio Holmes!

He's not really the great, great grandson of the fictional character Sherlock Holmes, but all the other kids seem to think he is. Now he's a detective whether he likes it or not. Still, he's creative, good at thinking through facts, and has a wicked smart best friend, Jinju. Together, they might make great detectives after all!

Chapter 1
It's Not That Easy Being Green

I don't really like green. You know what, I dislike green. I wouldn't say I hate green, but it's close. I have two favorite colors, blue and yellow. I know blue and yellow together make green. But to me, green is not blue and yellow, it's just green.

This might seem irrelevant at first. Maybe it is, because who knows how things might have turned out if I did like green. But it was due, at least in part, to my aversion to that hue that my career as a detective continued past my first, and what I had planned to be my only, case.

My mom knows about my color preferences, and she still gives me lots of green things, because they go well with my blue clothes, and they go well with my yellow clothes. She had just come back from shopping where she bought me a new backpack. But really anything new from my mom isn't new, because she likes to shop at vintage stores. That's where everything is really, really old, but it's new to my mom, so she calls it new.

The backpack she got me was, yes, green. It had a frog on it and the word Robin. My name wasn't Robin. My mom told me Robin was the nephew of Kermit. I kind of remember Kermit the Frog from *Sesame Street*. He thought it was tough to be green, and I can't blame him. But I was practically a baby then. Was this a baby backpack? And I don't remember him having a nephew.

So now I had a backpack I didn't want, and I had a problem. My mom expected

2

me to use it. I didn't want to hurt her feelings. But I didn't want to use a green backpack either. So I was sitting on the front step of my house, thinking about what to do. I was looking at the beautiful no longer green leaves, all orange and red and my favorite, yellow.

"Ratio!" I heard someone shout my name.

Coming up the street fast on a bike, a green bike, was my friend Jimmy-called-James. He liked green. He liked all colors. Jimmy-called-James was one of the best painters in my school. He would have said he was the best, not one of the best. Maybe he was. And a great painter couldn't dislike green. Plus it was his last name, Green, so I guess he kind of had to like it.

Jimmy-called-James skidded to a stop in my driveway.

"Ratio!" he said again.

"Hi Jimmy-called-James."

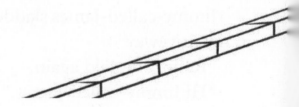

"Just James."

I said, "But your name's Jimmy."

"But I go by James."

"But your real name's Jimmy." His real name was Jimmy, I wasn't making that up. I guess that's what his birth certificate said. It was certainly the name he was registered under at school. I liked having Jimmy-called-James in my class on the first day of school. He got called in roll before me, and had to sort out that he didn't want to be called Jimmy, but instead James, and this always confused teachers. When they got to Holmes and I asked to be called Ratio instead of Horatio it seemed like nothing.

"But I go by James."

"But–"

"Ratio, stop it," he interrupted. "I need your help."

I figured his bike tires were low and he needed me to get out the pump or something. "Sure, what's up?"

"You have to get me reinstated in the Downtown Art Festival Competition."

How was I going to do that? Every year the city sponsored a Downtown Art Festival. Each school got to submit one painter for the big competition. Actually, two, one for kids up to third grade, and one for kids fourth through sixth. Those winners got to compete with all the other school winners in their age category. But I didn't know anything about being reinstated. I wasn't even sure what he meant.

"What do you mean?"

"I got kicked out for cheating. But I didn't do it, and you have to get me back in."

"Why me?" I asked.

"Madison told me how you helped Tommy with his cap. You're the best detective in school."

That again? This was Jinju's fault. She's my best friend, usually. But she'd told a story of how I was descended from Sherlock Holmes. Now I know he's not even real, but everyone at school seemed to believe it.

"Jimmy-called-James–"

"Just James!"

"James," I said, "I'm not really so good as you think."

"Please, Ratio," he begged. "Aren't you my friend?"

"Yeah."

"You're my only hope. Help me and I'll paint your bike to be the coolest bike ever."

He seemed so desperate. And I know how important that competition is to him. Jimmy-called-James thinks he's a great artist. He talks about how he was classically trained at La Coal Day Share Shay Wheat, or something. Jinju says it's supposed to be a French school, and I'm sure I'm spelling it not French like, but it's made up anyway. I met Jimmy in kindergarten. He was just Jimmy then, the James thing didn't start until second grade. Unless he went to an art preschool, he made the whole thing up.

Still, he really does believe he's the best artist, and he's sure he'll be a famous painter. He did win the citywide kindergarten through third grade competition last year, so maybe he's right. This competition means a ton to Jimmy-called-James.

How could I say no?

"All right," I said. "Tell me what happened."

"We can only paint our paintings at school, to make sure they're really ours."

"Okay."

"And we have to leave them there overnight."

"Uh-huh."

"Someone vandalized one of the paintings."

"Not yours?"

"No," he said. "Wilson Nym's painting."

Wilson was a fifth-grader. We'd met once or twice on the dodgeball court. He had a good arm, but couldn't dodge to save his life. He was usually one of the first ones out.

"What happened? Someone ripped it?"

"No, painted a blue stripe across it."

"He can't pick it off?"

"Not without picking off what's underneath it."

"This does sound bad for Wilson, but why were you kicked out?"

"I've been blamed for it!"

"Why does anyone think you did it?"

"It was my paint."

I asked, "Isn't your paint the same as everyone else's?"

"Not my blue. For this project I was experimenting with blue paint made from lapis lazuli."

"What's lapis lazuli?"

"It's a blue rock. In the old days, they

used to crush it and mix it with paint to make it blue."

"So someone used your special paint to ruin Wilson's picture."

He nodded. "It wasn't me, Ratio. You have to believe me."

I did believe him.

"You just hired yourself a detective."

"Thank you, Ratio."

"Now, who kicked you out?"

"Well, that's the other reason I thought you'd be the best detective for the job."

"Why? Who was it?" I asked.

Jimmy-called-James got a weird look, almost shy or something. He gulped.

"Your mom."

Chapter 2
Facts are Facts

That shouldn't have surprised me, because my mom is the art teacher at Longtides Elementary. But somehow I was surprised. Though probably, deep down, I had known all along who my adversary was likely to be. And because of the green backpack and the dislike of green I mentioned before, I think I was primed to pick a fight with her. So that's why I say my dislike of green led to me accepting my second case as a detective.

I was already upset with my mom about the backpack, so I probably should have known better than to try talking with her just then. But I didn't know better.

I stormed into the house.

"Hi Way!" I heard. It was my sister, Phelia. It sounds like highway, but she was really saying "Hi Ray." That's what my dad calls me, and Phelia does too. But she has a hard time saying her 'r' sounds.

She was standing in front of the pantry in the kitchen, stretching to get something too high for her. "Hey Phelia."

"Way!" she said. "Help me." She pointed to a box of baking soda.

I pulled it down off of the shelf and handed it to her. "Where's Mom?" I asked.

"In the backyawd," she said. Then she skipped off to her room still holding the box.

Mom was in her garden, picking the tomatoes that were already red.

"Hi handsome," she said when she saw me, "want to help me pick these?"

"No," I said. "Why didn't you tell me you kicked Jimmy-called-James out of the art competition?"

She looked into my eyes. "It was private. How did you hear?"

"He told me."

"Well, that's his business."

"Why did you do it? Why would you kick him out?"

"He ruined the painting of another boy."

"It wasn't Jimmy."

She sounded tired. "How do you know that?"

"He told me."

"Horatio, sometimes people don't tell the truth."

I knew that. It wasn't like I was an imbecile.

"But he is telling the truth."

"That's your opinion, honey."

"No," I said. "It's a fact."

"Can you prove it?" she asked. "And James saying he didn't do it isn't proof."

"Well, no. But you thinking he did do it is just your opinion."

"No, that's a fact."

"What's your proof?"

"It was done in a special paint that James made himself."

"That doesn't prove anything. Someone else could have used it."

"No," she said. "It's made with a slightly expensive rock, honey."

"Lapis lazuli. He told me."

"I keep it in a locked cabinet and only take it out when James has art class or when he's working on his painting at recess."

"Then even Jimmy-called-James couldn't have gotten to it."

"He could have made more at home. He has the lapis lazuli."

"Well, maybe you forgot to lock the cabinet."

"Horatio, I know he's your friend, but–"

"Isn't it possible you forgot?"

"Horatio! Facts are facts and opinions, until they are proven, are not. Now, we are done discussing this!"

That was a fact.

I stalked toward my room, but before I got there, I had an idea. I turned around and headed for the kitchen. As I passed Phelia's room I thought I heard a fizzing, but I didn't have time to investigate that. I already had a case.

In the kitchen I grabbed the phone and called Jinju. I hoped she was back from her camping trip. Seemed a bit cold for camping to me, but not, apparently, for the The family.

Jinju's father answered the phone. Good. They were back. I asked for Jinju and after a moment, she got on the phone.

"Hi Jinju. How was the trip?"

"Stupendous," she told me. "When we arrived on Friday, my father allowed me to select our tent's location and directional facing. I found level ground at higher elevation and chose a direction of slightly west of–"

I knew if I didn't stop her I would get every detail of the past two days of her life.

"Jinju. I'm sorry to interrupt. I want

to hear about it, but there's no time right now."

"Why not?"

"We have a case."

"A case? You mean as detectives?"

"Yeah."

"I was under the impression that had been a solitary endeavor."

"What?" I asked.

"I thought we weren't accepting more cases."

"I wasn't going to. But this was a friend in need."

"Which, according to a literal interpretation of an adage is a friend indeed. However, I conclude that you are the friend indeed, and not the friend in need."

I didn't know what she was talking about, so I explained the details of the case to her, including the conversation with my mom.

"Ratio," she said when I was done, "have you considered that Jimmy-called-

James may, in truth, be guilty?"

"He's not."

"Could your friendship with him be interfering with your objectivity?"

I thought for a second and figured out what she was talking about. Since Jimmy-called-James was my friend, was that clouding my judgment? Jinju had never taken to Jimmy-called-James. She thought he was haughty. When I asked her what that meant she told me it was disdainful. Eventually I figured out she was calling him stuck-up. Which he is.

"Maybe," I admitted. "But I still don't think he's guilty. It doesn't make sense."

"Why not?"

"Two reasons. You know how you say he's haughty?"

"He is."

"Yeah, and he's so haughty, he couldn't believe Wilson's painting might have been better than his. Why would he bother to wreck it?"

"You're saying he's too arrogant to be a saboteur?"

"Uh, sure."

"Plausible. What's the second reason?"

"If you were in the art room at school and about to destroy another painting, surrounded by all kinds of paints and paint thinner and whatever else, would you ruin that painting with the only thing in the room that had to come from you?"

"I don't follow."

"You've been in that room. Jimmy-called-James could have just grabbed a bottle of regular blue paint from a shelf and squeezed it out. Why would he use his own special blue paint which would make everyone suspect it was him?"

"Perhaps it was a crime of passion. He didn't take time to consider."

"Nah, then he would have ripped it or knocked the frame apart or something."

Jinju thought for a minute, and then said, "You make a compelling argument, but it isn't proof. What's our next step?"

"How early can you be at school tomorrow?"

It was right about then I heard my mom in Phelia's room saying, "How did you get baking soda?"

Chapter 3

Microscopic Examination

The teachers all get into school before the kids do. That makes sense. Otherwise, who would unlock all the doors for us? I walk to school. So does my mom. I got ready early, but still waited for her to leave. Then I left two minutes later. I didn't bring my new Robin the Frog backpack. I carried my old one, which was orange.

Jinju's mom dropped her at school early. I was going to have to face my mom to solve my case, so we went directly to the art room.

"Horatio? Jinju? Why are you here so

early?"

"Investigation, Mrs. Holmes," Jinju said.

I added, "We want to see the ruined painting. And the locked cabinet. And Jimmy's special paint."

Mom frowned. "I don't think this is a good idea."

"That's not fair, Mom. You said my opinion can't be a fact unless I prove it. But I can't do that if you won't let me see the evidence."

She thought about it. I didn't know what I was going to do if she refused. Luckily she didn't. "You're right, Horatio."

We got to see the ruined painting. It had a cloth covering it. I lifted the cloth and there it was. I don't know what it was supposed to be, even without the blue stripe. It didn't look like anything. But I know a lot of art doesn't look like anything and that doesn't mean it isn't good. The stripe was blue, but kind of a deep shade of it.

The locked cabinet was nothing special, just a big metal cabinet with double doors. Each had a handle and one of them had a lock. It would have been hard to break into it without denting or scratching the doors, and they were fine. No luck there.

Jimmy-called-James's paint was inside of it. And the shade was exactly the same as the blue stripe.

Otherwise, the art room looked like it always did this time of year. Lots of easels with covered paintings.

"Mrs. Holmes," Jinju asked, "are the paintings always covered with cloths?"

"Yes. So the competitors can't see one another's work."

"So Wilson's painting was covered. When was the vandalism discovered?"

"On Friday morning. Wilson came to art with the rest of his class. When he uncovered it, he saw the stripe."

I asked, "When had it last been uncovered before that?"

"He was working on it Thursday during recess."

A lot of the kids who competed each year gave up their recesses to work on their paintings.

"And was Jimmy-called-James here at recess on Thursday?"

"Of course. He's here everyday leading up to the competition."

"Thank you," I said, trying to sound objective, I think that was Jinju's word. "Please don't throw away the ruined painting. I'd like to see it again."

"Fine. But it doesn't leave this room." I could tell from Mom's tone that she was losing patience with our investigation. "By the way, the judges come right after school tomorrow. So if you're going to prove anything, you only have until then."

We walked out into the hall. I turned to Jinju.

"How do we know that stripe is Jimmy's paint?"

"It looked like the same shade."

"Couldn't someone else make a paint the same shade?"

"Without a sample of his paint? It seems unlikely."

"But possible."

I led us to Mr. Brighton's classroom. He teaches us science. He was setting up clay in the front of the room. He saw us enter.

"Jinju! Ratio! What's up?"

"Mr. B, we need your help. Do you have a microscope?" I asked.

"I'm sure I could get one from Mrs. Tarkleton. Why?"

"Jimmy-called-James has been accused of wrecking another boy's painting. We don't think he did it. We're out to prove he's innocent."

Mr. B didn't say anything. He just looked us both over and nodded a lot. He told us he could get one, but probably not immediately. I asked if he'd have it by recess, and he thought he could manage that.

I had a hard time paying much attention in class that morning. I kept trying to figure out who, when, how, and why? If it wasn't Jimmy-called-James, who was it? When did that person paint the stripe? How did they get the special paint? And why Wilson's painting and not all of the others?

I told Jimmy-called-James I was making progress, but he seemed pretty morose, which is very sad.

Finally recess arrived. We ran to Mr. B's room, and true to his word, he had the microscope. I asked if we could take it to the art room. Mr. B insisted on accompanying us, or the microscope, I'm not sure which. He also had the good idea to bring some slides.

Lots of kids were in the art room, working on their paintings. Jimmy-called-

James was there too. I guess he was confident we were going to prove him innocent and wanted to keep working on his. Wilson Nym was there too, and on his easel was a new painting.

While Mr. B and my mom said hi to one another I snuck behind Wilson.

This was not a new painting at all. The canvas was full. It looked like the Statue of Liberty but her back, like you were standing behind her. She was standing on a tall pedestal on an island. You could see the water all around the island. And in the water past her, where she would be looking if we could see her face, were a bunch of big ships: Battleships and gunboats. And at the bottom was a green rectangle. I couldn't figure what that was supposed to be.

"How did you paint that much that fast?" I asked.

"What?" Wilson noticed me and immediately covered his painting. He complained about me looking.

"Horatio is not in the competition, Wilson," my mother said. "But from now on, respect Mr. Nym's privacy, Horatio."

"Okay, sorry. But how could he have a new painting so fast?"

"Because of the irregularities, I have

allowed Wilson to bring a painting he has been working on at home."

Jimmy-called-James asked the obvious question, though I wished it had come from someone other than him. "How do you know it's his?"

"Both Wilson and his mother have given me their word. Normally I would not allow this, but given the circumstances . . ." Mom glared at Jimmy-called-James, and he backed behind his canvas.

My mom continued. "Mr. B tells me you came to investigate. Why don't you do so?"

Mr. B set up the microscope while Jinju and I took out slides. I went to the wrecked painting and scraped some of the blue paint off and placed it on the slide. Jinju put a glop of Jimmy-called-James's special paint on her slide. Then we looked at each through the microscope.

Of course they weren't going to look exactly the same, since one was wet and one was dry. But I was hoping they would look completely different.

In the wet slide, we could see the tiny pieces of lapis lazuli rock. With the microscope, the little flakes looked like crooked squares. I was sure we wouldn't see those squares on the other slide.

And at first we didn't, but I didn't really have the microscope focused right. Mr. B looked through and played with the fine adjustment. Sure enough, the squares were there. It was the same paint.

I admitted this to my mom. "I hope this puts an end to your investigation," she said.

"No," I said. "I'm not giving up yet."

Jimmy-called-James smiled when I said that. I think Mr. B did too. I'm not sure how Mom felt about it.

Chapter 4
Fleet Week

"I wish you'd seen Wilson's new painting."
I said to Jinju.

"I did."

"When?"

"While everyone was interested in
the microscope. I employed stealth."

"You go!"

"It's Fleet Week."

"What?"

"The painting, It's Fleet Week. In
May each year, several naval ships sail up
the Hudson River and dock in New York
City. People can tour them."

"How do you know that?"

Jinju shrugged. "My father subscribes to *The New York Times*."

"And you read it?"

"Most days."

"What if Wilson didn't paint that painting?"

"What do you mean?"

"He brought it from home. What if it's a painting he just had lying around? Look, his other painting was weird, I don't know what."

"Abstract?"

"Right! This one is definitely a real picture. Totally different. What if his first painting was bad, really bad."

Jinju asked, "Ghastly? Revolting? Gruesome?"

"Yes, yes, yes. Point made. So what if he ruined his own painting so that he could bring in this one? And framed Jimmy-called-James at the same time?"

"How did he get the special paint?"

"I don't know yet. Brainstorm with me."

"Okay. Then who did paint it?"

"I don't know. You'd think–"

I gasped. Suddenly I knew what that green rectangle was. And I knew I was right. Wilson Nym didn't paint that painting.

I hurried to the school office and borrowed a phone book. I jotted down an address. Jinju glanced at what I was writing.

She said, "I see we're visiting the Nyms after school today."

The Nyms were a pretty rich family, if their house told us anything. And when Mrs. Nym answered the door, that seemed to confirm it. She was big, I mean fat, and had a bunch of jewels all over.

Wilson wasn't home, but that was fine. I told Mrs. Nym that I was thinking the school newspaper should do an article on Wilson. I had just thought of that, so it wasn't a lie. I didn't say I was writing the article. Our school newspaper comes out once a month and tells us what we're having for hot lunch each day, and that's about it. But it was possible that it could have an article, and I had that thought. Mrs. Nym was enthusiastic about the idea.

"Rumor has it that his new painting has something to do with New York. Has Wilson ever been there?" I asked.

"Yes," Mrs. Nym answered. "Just this past May. We had to take Wilson out of school for two weeks, but William, that's Wilson's father, had a conference there and we decided it would be a wonderful family time."

Jinju said, "I was born right near there. In New Jersey."

"Oh, you poor child!"

"Why?"

"New Jersey is simply not the place to be."

I asked, "Have you ever been there?"

"Certainly not," she was offended. "As I said, it is not the place to be."

I noticed lots of paintings in the Nym home. "Are you an art collector?"

"Why, yes. William and I love to broaden our collection of aht." It was weird how she said art without an 'r' sound. I wondered if she had the same speech problems as Phelia. I had always figured Phelia would outgrow it, but maybe some people never did.

"Does Wilson collect art?"

"He just began to in New York. William and I collect masters, but Wilson can't afford aht like that. He did buy several paintings from less proven ahtists selling wares before the Metropolitan Museum."

She showed us Wilson's room, and sure enough there were a few paintings here and there. I also spotted a nail in one wall, a nail that could have once held a painting. Maybe even a painting that was currently on an easel at school. Of course, I knew an extra nail wasn't proof of anything.

As Mrs. Nym was showing us out, Jinju asked, "Just out of curiosity, ma'am, did you visit the Statue of Liberty while you were there?"

"Yes," she said. "Wilson and I took the ferry from Manhattan one morning."

"Thank you for everything, Mrs. Nym," I said.

She closed the door and Jinju turned to me. "Do we know anything?"

"We know he didn't paint that painting."

"Can we prove it?"

"I'll get back to you on that."

Chapter 5

The Scientific Method

I arrived at school early again the next day, and as soon as Mrs. Fry opened the library, I started my research on the Statue of Liberty. I knew I had to prove that Wilson Nym did not paint that picture. I still didn't know how I could prove Jimmy-called-James wasn't the vandal, but I was hoping an idea would come to me on that one.

Jinju joined me in the library as soon as she got to school, but the bell rang for class before we found anything useful. Conclusive is what Jinju said.

So we returned to the library at recess.

"This is fascinating," Jinju said.

"What? Did you find something?"

"Yes. Did you know that Bartholdi, the man who sculpted the statue, came over to New York to pick the location? He picked Fort Wood on Bedloe's Island, and envisioned the lady facing east across the harbor."

"Jinju, that's very interesting. And completely unhelpful! Come on!"

"Sorry."

The bell rang for lunch. I was hungry, but I didn't have time. Mrs. Fry told us to go, but we begged to skip lunch and stay. The judges came after school today. If we didn't solve this now, we weren't going to. Mrs. Fry didn't seem happy about it, but she let us keep working and called the office to tell them where we were.

I looked at the clock. Lunch period was almost over. I was searching website after website on the library computer, but coming up with nothing. I was almost out of time.

I closed my eyes, trying to envision Wilson's Fleet Week painting. I thought I was just like Bartholdi envisioning his statue standing on an island that had nothing at the time.

"Wait a second," I said. "Which way did you say Lady Liberty faces?"

I knew Jinju would remember. She never forgets anything. "East."

"I need a map of the harbor."

Jinju started to search for one on the internet, but just then lunch period ended.

"You kids have to get back to class," Mrs. Fry said. We knew she was right. We tried to convince her anyway, but she was not going to let us stay.

After lunch we had science class. But Mr. B had a computer in his room. Maybe he'd let us finish our research. I knew we were close. I just needed that map. I could feel it inside of me.

"Mr. B," I pleaded, "can we please use the computer?"

He frowned. "Is this about your investigation, Ratio?"

"Yes, but after school today–"

"Ratio, I'm sorry, but this is science class. I appreciate what you're trying to do, but we need to learn science."

"But what if it is science, Mr. B?" Jinju asked.

"How so, Jinju?"

"We will be using the computer as part of the scientific method. Ratio and I have made observations and we have formulated a hypothesis. While we can't perform a formal experiment, we will use the computer to collect data allowing us to accept or reject our hypothesis."

Man, sometimes you just had to love Jinju. I wasn't sure which way Mr. B would decide, but she gave us a chance.

"All right, Miss The, I accept your explanation. Verify or disprove your hypothesis."

Yes! We ran to the computer. I gave Jimmy-called-James the thumbs up sign. We just might make it in time.

Jinju brought up the map of New York Harbor. I found Liberty Island, what was once called Bedloe's Island. I checked the compass rose. I was right! "Yes!" I shouted. Mr. B didn't appreciate that. I apologized.

I showed Jinju what I was thinking. But she had a concern. We checked another website and Jinju sent an e-mail.

She said, "The only problem is how soon will they respond?"

There was no response when science class ended. And without a reply to our e-mail, all of our work might have been for nothing.

Chapter 6

Prove It!

School ended. Jinju headed straight for the library where she promised to dutifully wait for any response to our e-mail. I went to the art room.

One of the judges had already arrived. His name was Mr. Herrick, and he was the art teacher at another school. Two more judges were left to arrive. I hoped the e-mail would get here first. But the second judge came and still no Jinju. Then the third arrived.

They were about to start judging paintings. All of the kids who had painted something were in the room, including Jimmy-called-James. He kept looking at me, waiting for me to do something. I couldn't wait any longer.

"Stop!" I cried. Everyone turned to look at me. My mom didn't look happy.

"Horatio Holmes," she started, but I didn't let her finish.

"Wilson Nym didn't paint that painting. And I can prove it!"

The judges were shocked. My mother was shocked. The kids in the room were shocked.

"Horatio," my mom said. "This has gone on long enough. I've been patient with your investigation, but now you are making accusations. I think you should leave."

"I'm sorry to intrude, Mrs. Holmes," came a voice from behind me. "But I think you should hear him out." It was Mr. B. I don't know when he arrived, but I was so glad he was there.

Mom insisted we call Wilson's mother before I had my say. That was fine with me, because it was all the longer Jinju had to get that e-mail back.

Mrs. Nym said she would be right over. Everyone in the art room felt pretty weird waiting. The judges went ahead and looked over the paintings from the kindergarten through third grade group, since there wasn't any controversy there.

My mom was really embarrassed. Her look told me what she was thinking. I'd better have something really good, really conclusive as Jinju would say, or I was going to be in big, big trouble.

Mrs. Nym didn't take nearly long enough to arrive because Jinju still wasn't there. And now everyone was looking at me. Jimmy-called-James had hope in his eyes. Wilson Nym and his mother had something much less pleasant in theirs. And Mom's eyes were the scariest of all.

I started. "Wilson, your painting is of

Fleet Week in New York, right?"

"Yes."

"The ships passing the Statue of Liberty?"

"Obviously."

"And how did you, I mean, did you see this happen?"

"Yes."

"How?"

"What do you mean how?" Wilson was annoyed. "I was there. My family went to New York City last May."

"Of course. And this picture, this was the view you had?"

"Yes."

"This exact view."

"Yes."

"From this angle, with this–"

"Horatio!" Mom shouted. I think she knew I was stalling.

"Did you paint this while you were at the spot, Wilson?" I asked.

"No. I memorized it."

"Entirely? All those details? No sketch."

"Maybe a little one, to remember details."

"Can you bring that sketch?" I asked.

"No. I don't know where it is anymore. But this painting is exactly what I saw."

"Exactly?"

Mr. B nudged me. "I think you should

make your next point, Ratio."

"Mrs. Nym, where all did you visit on your trip?"

"What do you mean?"

"Where all did you go? Just Manhattan? Anywhere else?"

"We went to Brooklyn, which is also part of New York City. And we took the ferry to the Statue of Liberty."

"And that's all?"

"Yes. Why are we here?"

"Hold on," I said. "Wilson, you agree. Those are all the places you went?"

"Yes already!"

I pulled a paper I had printed at the library out of my backpack, the orange one.

"It's interesting," I said. "Your picture shows the Statue of Liberty from behind. We see her back."

No one could argue. We could see the painting.

I continued. "The Statue of Liberty,

of course, faces east. You can see for yourself."

I passed around the paper on the history of the Statue of Liberty from the U.S. Parks Service website. It was true that Lady Liberty faces east.

"So if she faces east, and we're looking at her back, then when you saw this view, you must have been . . ."

"West," Mr. B finished my sentence for me.

"Exactly," I said. I pulled another paper from my backpack. It was one I had printed in Mr. B's room. "I have here a map of New York Harbor. This is Liberty Island. And this is west."

I pointed. Everyone looked.

"What this means," I said, my heart pounding so loud I was amazed anyone could hear me talking over the sound of it, "is the only place you could have had this view of the Statue of Liberty from the west is in Liberty State Park. And that is in a place that both you and your mother just told us you were not ever at. New Jersey."

Eyes were wide all around the room. Wilson stammered and wrung his hands together. Mrs. Nym was angry.

"Wait one second!" she cried. "We visited the Statue of Liberty. We were on the island, and you can certainly walk behind her on the island. He saw the view from there."

"No ma'am," said one of the judges whose name I later learned was Ms. Exton. "This picture is not from a view on the island. You can see the water and then the island. I think the boy's right."

"Then Wilson must have seen this view from the boat, the ferry boat that took us to the island."

Ms. Exton said, "Now that's a possibility."

"No it isn't." It was Jinju. She was standing in the doorway with one more piece of paper. The e-mail had finally arrived.

"This is an e-mail from Yolanda Harvey who works at the Circle Line, the company that runs the ferries to and from the Statue of Liberty. As you can read here, I asked her if the ferries ever run behind the Statue, and you can also read her reply. They always go in front of her, never behind."

"That's true," Mr. Herrick said. "I used to live in New York, and that's absolutely true. I remember now."

Wilson screamed. "I swear I painted this canvas."

"That's true," I said. "You painted on that canvas, but only that green rectangle at the bottom. You bought this painting on your trip to New York, and you painted over the name of the actual artist."

"Mommy," Wilson squeaked.

Mrs. Nym turned toward him. "You lied to me, young man. You told me you painted this scene. You lied."

I tried to finish up my whole argument. "Wilson knew his painting wasn't any good, so he vandalized it himself. He was hoping you would let him bring one from home, so he could bring this one that he didn't actually paint himself!"

The room burst into talk. There was shouting, there was crying, there was laughing. Until my mom shouted, "Everyone quiet!"

We were all silent at once.

Mom said, "Wilson, you cheated, and I am disqualifying your painting. I think Horatio has presented ample evidence that you did not paint this yourself."

I did it!

"But . . ."

Uh-oh. Hadn't I done it?

"This in no way proves that Wilson vandalized his own painting. And given the paint is the lapis lazuli paint that James made himself, I see no reason to reinstate his painting."

I hadn't done it. I saw Jimmy-called-James deflate.

Think fast, Ratio. That's what I told myself. Don't give up. Think fast.

"Wait! I've got it!" I shouted. Again, everyone was silent.

"Fact!" I said. "Wilson covered his painting with the cloth before he left during recess on Thursday. Fact, it was uncovered again during art class on Friday morning and had a blue stripe on it. Fact, that blue stripe was the special paint made by Jimmy-called-James."

"Just James," Jimmy-called-James said.

"Whatever. Go back to recess Thursday. Jimmy–"

"James!"

"Whatever! Jimmy-called-James was here painting. His special paint was out of the locked cabinet because he was here. Isn't it possible that anyone could have gotten a brush full of his special paint at recess on Thursday?"

My mom shook her head. "I don't know about that, Horatio."

"Are you saying it's not even possible?"

"It's possible."

"So it's possible that Wilson painted that stripe on Thursday at recess, then covered the painting himself."

"I did not!" Wilson cried.

Jinju said, "Wilson, you haven't really proven yourself a man of his word."

"Mom," I said, "it's possible."

"Yes," Mom said. "It's possible. But I don't think so."

"You don't think so, but that's your opinion. It's not a fact. Facts are facts and opinions, until they are proven, are not."

Oh, my mom was mad at me. I had just disagreed with her, challenged her in front of a lot of people, including grown-ups. I could tell she was mad. And somehow, though parents always want you to listen and remember what they say, this time I don't think she liked that I remembered what she had told me quite so well. Weird.

She was quiet for a long time. Everyone was waiting to see what she was going to say.

"James," she finally said, "I do not know for a fact that it was you who painted the blue stripe on Wilson's painting. Therefore, I am reinstating your painting into the competition."

I did it! I did it! I might be in a lot of trouble tonight, but I did it!

Jimmy-called-James gave me a huge hug. I didn't like it, but he probably wasn't thinking straight. He told me I could call him Jimmy-called-James and he wouldn't even correct me anymore. The three judges patted me on the back. And Mr. B said, "I'm proud of you, Ratio. That took courage and intelligence."

After a lot of cleansing breaths my mom said, "I'm proud of you too, son."

When Mom came home from school that afternoon, I could tell she wasn't ready to talk to me, and I left her alone. But Laura, our nanny, didn't leave, so I guess Mom didn't go get Phelia either.

About an hour later, a little before Dad came home, I was sitting on the front step holding my Robin the Frog backpack, thinking maybe if I used it tomorrow Mom would stop being mad. She came out. I didn't move or say anything. Mom sat down beside me and wrapped her arms around me.

"Horatio," she said, "you don't have to use the green backpack."

I don't know how she does it, but sometimes Mom can read my mind.

Questions for Discussion

1. Do you think Ratio took on a second case because Jimmy-called-James is his friend or because somewhere in his brain he was upset with his mom? What makes you think that?

2. Ratio's mom talks about facts and opinions. If something is possible, but unproven, is it a fact or an opinion? What if something has happened, but you don't know that it happened for sure? Then is it a fact or an opinion?

3. Lapis lazuli was an important stone for making blue paint before the rise of synthetic dyes. Where was lapis lazuli mined? How did painters get it, even those who lived far from where it was mined?

4. If blue paints needed lapis lazuli to make them blue, how were other paints colored? Before synthetic dyes, what was used to get different reds or yellows or greens or anything else?

5. Jinju describes Wilson's first painting, the one which was vandalized, as ghastly or revolting or gruesome. Do these words all make you imagine the painting in the same way? Or do they mean slightly different things? What are some other words you might use to describe a painting that wasn't any good?

6. Do you think Ratio was wrong to tell Mrs. Nym that he was thinking of writing an article for the school newspaper about Wilson?

Letters to Ratio

Dear Mr. Holmes,

How can you not like green? So if you prefer the leaves when they turn colors, what do you do all summer? You just go around with your eyes closed? Don't you fall down a lot?

Sincerely,
Itanza T.

Dear Itanza,

No. It isn't that green upsets me. I just don't really like it. But I don't hide from summer. I must see the green leaves, I just don't think much about them at the time.

I really notice the leaves when they are prettier colors, or at least colors I prefer. But I don't have my eyes closed the rest of the time.

Your friend,
Ratio

Dear Ratio Holmes,

What do you call your mother when you are in

art class? Do you call her Mom because she's your mom or do you call her Mrs. Holmes because she's your teacher?

My mom is a Physical Education teacher at my school. When I am in P.E. class, I call her Coach like the other kids do.

Curious,
Bryan O.

Dear Bryan,

I am like you. I call my mom Mrs. Holmes when I'm in her class, like the other kids. When I was in first grade, I had a tougher time remembering that and sometimes called her Mom.

It's okay, because all my classmates know she's my mom. What they find funny isn't what I call her, but what she calls me. All the other teachers call me Ratio, but my mom only calls me Horatio.

Your friend,
Ratio (or Horatio)

Dear Ratio Holmes and Jinju The,

I was visiting my grandmother in a different state and at the grocery store we saw my school librarian, Ms. Sommes. Except when I said hi, she insisted she didn't know me and had never been to my school. She wasn't related to anyone in my city!

Then I remembered a time I had been to the school library and Ms. Sommes hadn't remembered what book I had checked out the week before. Do you think maybe Ms. Sommes is just one of a bunch of clones? Could you come investigate and find out if I'm right?

Freaked out,
Maria P.

Dear Maria,

As for Ms. Sommes forgetting which book you checked out, I don't think that's evidence that she was replaced by a clone. It would be pretty amazing if a librarian could remember every book that everyone checked out.

I asked Jinju about the person you saw in a different city. She said there is some research that people who aren't related could look so much alike you can't tell them apart at first. People like that are called doppelgängers. Jinju also said the research shows that sometimes people look enough alike that we think they look the same and if we really looked at them more closely, we would start to see differences.

Hope this helps.
Your friend,

Ratio

About the Author

Horatio Holmes has grown a lot since his days at Longtides Elementary. Since then he learned to play the bugle (badly), worked as a writer of competitive mathematics problems, even acted in *Hamlet* playing the very character for whom he was named.

In other ways, he's still the same as he ever was: an avid reader, a pursuer of justice, and someone who likes his hot dogs with mustard.